Captain
Mac

Written by Russell Punter

Illustrated by Paul Nicholls

How this book works

The story of **Captain Mac** has been written for you to read with your child. You take turns to read:

You read these words.

Captain Mac is busy.
He sails at half past ten.
But he still needs to find a crew.

"Can I get
ten men?"

5

Your child reads these words.

You don't have to finish the story in one session. If your child is getting tired, put a marker in the page and come back to it later.

You can find out more about helping your child with this book, and with reading in general, on pages 30-31.

Captain Mac

Turn the page to start the story.

Captain Mac is busy.
He sails at half past ten.
But he still needs to find a crew.

"Can I get
ten men?"

"I can be the cook," says Tom.
"Look out, or you'll get wet.
I can catch our supper."

I can get it
in a net.

"Stop that hungry rat!" cries Mac.
Ron has the pet for that.
"My cat will do the job," he cries.

"A cat can
get a rat."

"Who can clean the ship?" asks Mac.
"Right now it looks a wreck."
"Don't worry, Captain Mac,"
  says Ned.

I can mop
a deck.

"Who can help us find our way?"
Mac gives his charts a tap.
"I know which one to use,"
    says Nat.

I can pick a map.

Soon Mac has found nine sailors.
One more and he can stop.
"I can climb the mast,"
        says Rick.

Can I get up on top?

15

Now Rick is feeling dizzy,
He has to come down quick.
A sailor's life is not for him,
he's leaving.

Rick is sick.

A girl runs up. "I'm Pam," she cries.
She's on board with a hop.
"I'd like a job."

"Let's see," says Mac.

Pam, get up on top!

Pam scrambles up the rigging.
"The job is yours," shouts Mac.
"Get ready for the journey, lass."

"Run, kid.
Run and pack!"

"My crew's complete,"
beams Captain Mac.
"And every one's a gem.
The clock has struck,
the tide is right."

Puzzle 1

Match the speech bubbles to the pictures.

A

B

C

D

Puzzle 2

Choose the right word to complete the sentence.

1.

Can I get ten ....?

men	den	pen

2.

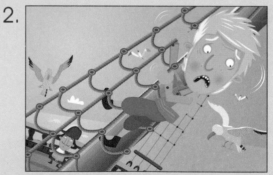

Rick is ....

tick	sick	pick

3.

Pam, get up on ....

| mop | pop | top |

4.

Run and ....

| rack | pack | sack |

Puzzle 3

Look at the pictures, read the sentences, then say whether they are true or false.

1. **I can mop.**

2. **I am sad.**

3. **I am sick.**

4. **I am on top.**

Answers to puzzles

Puzzle 1

1. I can mop a deck. – C
2. I can pick a map. – D
3. I can get it in a net. – A
4. A cat can get a rat. – B

Puzzle 2

1. Can I get ten <u>men</u>?
2. Rick is <u>sick</u>.
3. Pam, get up on <u>top</u>.
4. Run and <u>pack</u>.

Puzzle 3

1. True
2. False
3. True
4. False

Guidance notes

Usborne Very First Reading is a series of books, specially developed for children who are learning to read. In the early books in the series, you and your child take turns to read, and your child steadily builds the knowledge and confidence to read alone.

The words for your child to read in **Captain Mac** introduce these eight letters or letter-combinations:

g	o	c	k	ck	e	u	r

(Note that in this story, **c**, **k** and **ck** all have the same sound.) These are often among the first letters that children learn to read at school. Later books in the series gradually introduce more letters, sounds and spelling patterns, while reinforcing the ones your child already knows.

You'll find lots more information about the structure of the series, advice on helping your child with reading, extra practice activities and games on the Very First Reading website,[*] **www.usborne.com/veryfirstreading**

[*]US readers go to **www.veryfirstreading.com**

questions and answers

Why do I need to read with my child?
Sharing stories and taking turns makes
reading an enjoyable and fun activity for
children. It also helps them to develop
confidence and reading stamina, and to take
part in an exciting story using very few words.

- **When is a good time to read?**
Choose a time when you are both relaxed, but
not too tired, and there are no distractions.
Only read for as long as your child wants to –
you can always try again another day.

- **What if my child gets stuck?**
Don't simply read the problem word yourself,
but prompt your child and try to find the right
answer together. Similarly, if your child makes
a mistake, go back and look at the word
together. Don't forget to give plenty of praise
and encouragement.

- **We've finished, now what do we do?**
It's a good idea to read the story several times
to give your child more practice and confidence.
Then you can try reading **The Dressing-Up
Box** at the same level or, when your child is
ready, go on to Book 3 in the series.

Edited by Jenny Tyler, Lesley Sims
and Mairi Mackinnon

First published in 2011 by Usborne Publishing Ltd., Usborne House,
83-85 Saffron Hill, London EC1N 8RT, England. www.usborne.com
Copyright © 2011 Usborne Publishing Ltd.

7560992